A COLONY OF
RABBITS

by Danielle Denega

Children's Press®
An imprint of Scholastic Inc.

**A special thank-you to
the team at the Cincinnati Zoo & Botanical Garden
for their expert consultation.**

Library of Congress Cataloging-in-Publication Data
Names: Denega, Danielle, author.
Title: A colony of rabbits / by Danielle Denega.
Description: First edition. | New York, NY : Children's Press, an imprint of Scholastic Inc., 2023. | Includes index.
Audience: Ages 5–7. | Audience: Grades K–1.
Summary: "Next set in the Learn About series about animal groups"—Provided by publisher.
Identifiers: LCCN 2022025174 (print) | LCCN 2022025175 (ebook) | ISBN 9781338853377 (library binding)
ISBN 9781338853384 (paperback) | ISBN 9781338853414 (ebk)
Subjects: LCSH: Rabbits—Juvenile literature. | Rabbits—Behavior—Juvenile literature. | Rabbits—Nomenclature
(Popular)—Juvenile literature. | BISAC: JUVENILE NONFICTION / Animals / General
JUVENILE NONFICTION / Animals / Rabbits
Classification: LCC QL737.L32 D464 2023 (print) | LCC QL737.L32 (ebook) | DDC 599.32—dc23/eng/20220613
LC record available at https://lccn.loc.gov/2022025174
LC ebook record available at https://lccn.loc.gov/2022025175

10 9 8 7 6 5 4 3 2 1   23 24 25 26 27

Printed in China   62
First edition, 2023

Book design by Kimberly Shake

Photos ©: cover: Gary K Smith/Alamy Images; 4–5: Mike Powles/Getty Images; 8–9: Donald M. Jones/Minden Pictures;
10–11: Roger Tidman/FLPA/Minden Pictures; 11 top: www.marekszczepanek.pl/Getty Images; 12–13: stanley45/Getty Images;
14–15: Dorling Kindersley ltd/Alamy Images; 16–17: st-design/Getty Images; 18–19: Donald M. Jones/Minden Pictures; 20–21:
Ivan Kuzmin/Science Source; 22–23: Cyril Ruoso/Biosphoto; 24–25: shanelinkcom/Getty Images; 26–27: Sylvain Cordier/
Biosphoto; 28 top: Maia Kennedy/Alamy Images; 29 bottom: Lou Perrotti/RWP Zoo/Flickr; 30 bottom: Yann Avril/Biosphoto.

All other photos © Shutterstock.

TABLE OF
CONTENTS

INTRODUCTION
What Is a Colony of Rabbits? . . . 4

CHAPTER 1
Do All Rabbits Live in Groups? . . . 6

CHAPTER 2
Where Do Wild Rabbits Live? . . . 12

CHAPTER 3
All Ears . . . 16

CHAPTER 4
Rabbit Food . . . 20

CHAPTER 5
Baby Bunnies . . . 24

CONCLUSION
Fluffy Friends . . . 28

Rabbits at Risk . . . 29

Pet Rabbits . . . 30

Glossary . . . 31

Index/About the Author . . . 32

Many animals form groups for different reasons. Some animals travel together in groups. Some form groups to protect one another. Groups of different animals also have many different names. A group of wild rabbits is called a **colony**. Wild rabbits live all around the world except for Antarctica. Rabbits are **mammals**. They are one of the most common animals in the world.

In parts of Canada, a group of wild rabbits is called a fluffle!

Scientists have discovered 29 **species**, or types, of rabbits.

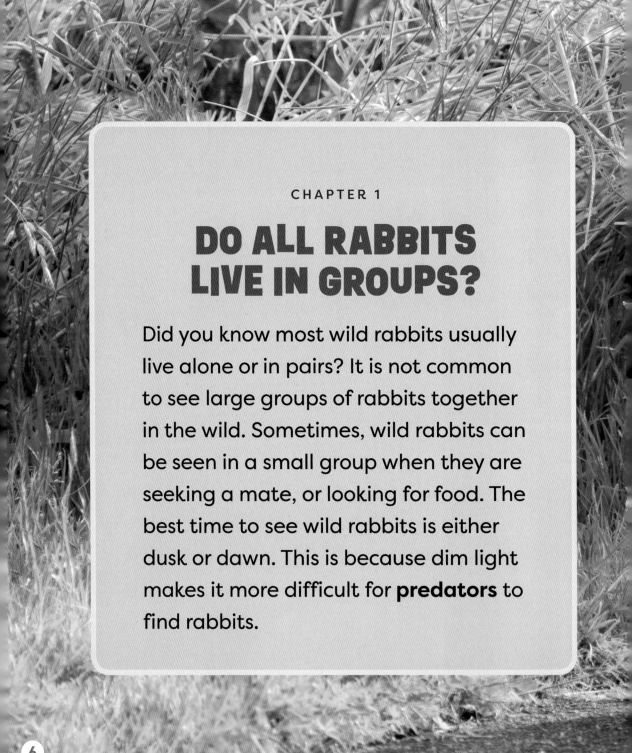

CHAPTER 1

DO ALL RABBITS LIVE IN GROUPS?

Did you know most wild rabbits usually live alone or in pairs? It is not common to see large groups of rabbits together in the wild. Sometimes, wild rabbits can be seen in a small group when they are seeking a mate, or looking for food. The best time to see wild rabbits is either dusk or dawn. This is because dim light makes it more difficult for **predators** to find rabbits.

Wild rabbit predators include coyotes, foxes, and wolves.

These eastern cottontail rabbits are munching on grass together.

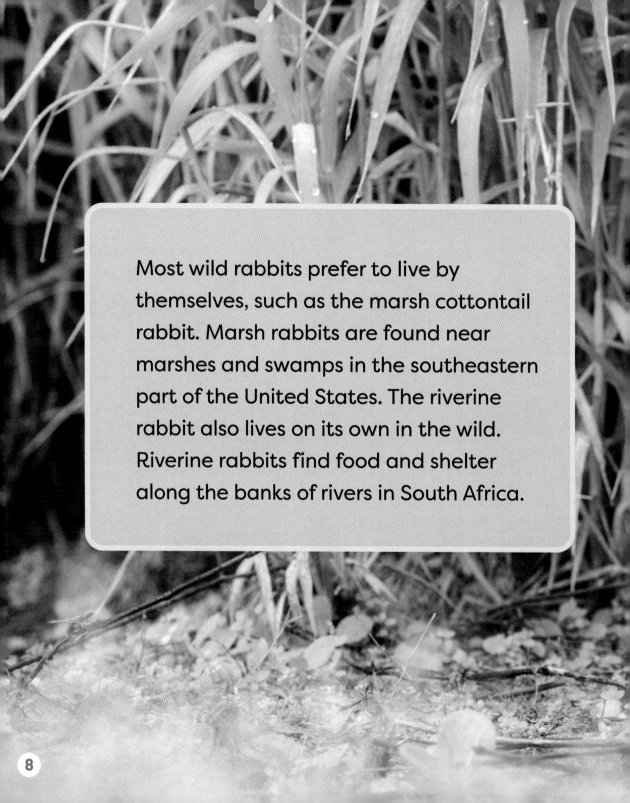

Most wild rabbits prefer to live by themselves, such as the marsh cottontail rabbit. Marsh rabbits are found near marshes and swamps in the southeastern part of the United States. The riverine rabbit also lives on its own in the wild. Riverine rabbits find food and shelter along the banks of rivers in South Africa.

Rabbits rub their chins on leaves to mark their territory. Their scent tells other rabbits to stay away.

Marsh rabbits often dive underwater to escape from predators.

There is one type of wild rabbit that likes to live in a large group: the European rabbit. As many as 20 European rabbits might live together in a colony. European rabbits live on nearly every continent in the world. They are also the most popular **domesticated** rabbit.

When a rabbit thumps its back legs on the ground, it is telling its colony that danger is nearby.

About 200 million wild European rabbits live in Australia.

European rabbits usually live in short grassland areas.

CHAPTER 2

WHERE DO WILD RABBITS LIVE?

Wild rabbits often live underground in tunnels called **burrows**. Some rabbits dig their own burrows by using their front feet and nails to loosen the dirt before their back legs kick it away. Living underground offers them a safe place to sleep and raise their babies. Some rabbit colonies live in an underground home called a warren. Within a **warren**, there is more than one burrow. There are also nests inside a warren.

These baby cottontail rabbits are safely snuggled inside their burrow.

Rabbit nests are made from grass, moss, and fur from the mother rabbit's body.

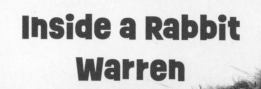

Inside a Rabbit Warren

ENTRANCE
Rabbits create a main entry to a burrow on a gentle slope of land.

NEST
This part of a burrow is where baby rabbits are born and fed by their mother.

BOLTHOLE
Rabbits use boltholes to quickly escape from danger.

BURROW
Rabbits dig tunnels or holes in the ground as a safe place to live.

CHAPTER 3

ALL EARS

Rabbits are easy to identify! They are known for their long ears, which they use to hear predators coming. Rabbits have large, powerful back legs that allow them to hop. Their soft fur can be shades of white, beige, gray, black, and brown. In Asia, there are even rabbits with black stripes!

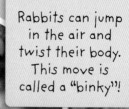

Rabbits can jump in the air and twist their body. This move is called a "binky"!

This lop-eared rabbit's ears hang down to the side.

A Rabbit's Body

EARS

Most rabbits have ears that stand up. They have a strong sense of hearing.

EYES

Rabbits have big eyes that sit high up on their heads. This gives them a wider range of vision.

NOSE

Rabbits wiggle their noses to help them breathe and smell.

MOUTH

Inside their mouths, rabbits have rows of teeth designed for chomping and chewing grasses and twigs.

HEAD

Rabbits will turn their heads toward an unusual sound or movement.

FORELIMB

The front legs of a rabbit are weaker than its hindlimbs.

CHAPTER 4

RABBIT FOOD

All rabbits are **herbivores**. Their diet mainly consists of grasses, herbs, and clover. When it is cold outside, wild rabbits eat dry twigs, bark, seeds, and grains. Rabbits also enjoy eating parsley, cabbage, and even flowers. Rabbits use two sets of teeth called **incisors** to bite and chew plants.

The eastern cottontail rabbit is solitary, or lives alone.

Rabbits' teeth keep growing throughout their lives.

As gross as it seems, wild rabbits eat some of their own poop. The plants that rabbits eat are hard for them to **digest.** At night, their bodies release soft, green pellets, or balls, made of food that wasn't entirely digested. They eat these pellets again so that they get even more nutrients from their food! During the day, rabbits produce hard, dry, brown pellets, which they do not eat.

Carrots contain sugar, so eating too many will actually upset a rabbit's stomach.

This European rabbit is eating its own pellets.

CHAPTER 5

BABY BUNNIES

Most people refer to rabbit babies as bunnies, but they are actually called kittens, or kits! A female rabbit often gives birth multiple times in a single year. There can be as many as seven kittens in a **litter**. At birth, kittens cannot see and have no fur. A litter is completely dependent on its mother for food and protection. At around 10 days old, a kitten will open its eyes for the first time.

Mother rabbits don't actually visit their babies very often. They only go to feed their young once or twice a day.

The rabbit kittens in this litter cannot yet open their eyes.

At first, newborn kittens' only source of food is their mother's milk. By the time kittens are around 18 days old, they begin to leave the burrow. During the day, young rabbits will nibble on wild grasses and other plants. At night, they still drink their mother's milk. Kittens stay near their family's burrow until they are about five weeks old. After that, they go into the wild by themselves.

Some people believe that if you say "rabbit, rabbit" on the first day of every month, you'll have good luck all year.

This young European rabbit has come out of its burrow.

The New England cottontail rabbit is sometimes called a brush rabbit or wood rabbit.

CONCLUSION

FLUFFY FRIENDS

Now you know more about wild rabbits and colonies of rabbits. Maybe you'll be lucky enough to see a group of wild rabbits together. Perhaps you'll spot a wild rabbit family or a wild rabbit alone in your own yard!

Rabbits at Risk

No matter where they're found, all wild rabbits need to be protected. Many types are disappearing from the wild. In fact, nearly half of the world's rabbit species are threatened or **endangered**. Many rabbits are **prey** for many other, larger animals. They are also threatened by humans, who destroy rabbit **habitats** by creating farms and putting up buildings. One simple way you can help protect rabbits is to give them a place to find shelter. Create piles of fallen branches and brush in your own yard or neighborhood park, which allows them to hide safely.

This New England cottontail family is being cared for at a zoo.

Pet Rabbits

Many people keep domesticated rabbits as pets. It is always important to be very gentle when handling rabbits. Their bodies are fragile! Pet rabbits can live in a cage called a hutch. They need proper food to be healthy and happy. Their nails should be trimmed, and their fur needs to be brushed often. Pet rabbits should be given small areas in which they can dig, just as they would in the wild.

When pet rabbits rearrange and organize their hutch, it is called bunching.

Rabbits can make great family pets.

Glossary

burrow (BUR-oh) a tunnel or hole in the ground made or used by a rabbit or other animal

colony (KAH-luh-nee) a large group of animals that live together

digest (dye-JEST) to break down food so that it can be absorbed by the blood and used by the body

domesticated (duh-MES-ti-kay-ted) a tamed animal that can live with or be used by people

endangered (en-DAYN-jurd) an animal or plant that is at risk of becoming extinct

habitat (HAB-i-tat) the place where an animal or a plant is usually found

herbivore (HUR-buh-vor) an animal that eats plants

incisor (in-SYE-zur) a kind of tooth in the front of the mouth that is used for cutting

litter (LIT-ur) a number of baby animals that are born at the same time to the same mother

mammal (MAM-uhl) a warm-blooded animal with a backbone; female mammals produce milk to feed their young

predator (PRED-uh-tur) an animal that lives by hunting other animals for food

prey (pray) an animal that is hunted by another animal for food

species (SPEE-sheez) a group of related animals or plants

warren (WOR-uhn) a group of underground tunnels where rabbits breed and live

Index

Bodies, 16–19, 30
boltholes, 15
bunching, 30
burrows, 12–15, 26–27

Colonies
defined, 4
living alone or in pairs compared to, 6–9, 21
number of rabbits in, 10
other names for, 5
reasons for forming, 6
types of rabbits in, 10–11

Diets, 20–26
digestion, 22
domesticated animals, 10, 30

Ears, 16–18
endangered animals, 29
eyes, 18, 24–25

Fur, 13, 16, 24, 30

Groups of rabbits. See colonies

Habitats, 8–15, 29
herbivores, 20
hutches, 30

Incisors, 20

Jumping, 16, 19

Kittens (baby rabbits), 24–27
in burrows, 12–14, 26–27
diet of, 24–26
number per litter, 24

Legs, 10, 12, 16–19
litters, 24–25

Mammals, 4

Nests, 12–14

Pellets, 22–23
pet rabbits, 10, 30
predators, 6–7, 9, 16
prey, 29

Species, 5

Teeth, 18, 20–21
territories, 9

Warrens, 12–15

ABOUT THE AUTHOR

Danielle Denega is the author of more than 50 books for young readers. She lives in Connecticut, where she has a hopping good time hanging out with her husband and daughters.